THE BIGGEST LIES EVER!

Alison Hawes

First Flight

Titles in First Flight

Badger Publishing Limited
15 Wedgwood Gate, Pin Green Industrial Estate,
Stevenage, Hertfordshire SG1 4SU
Telephone: 01438 356907. Fax: 01438 747015
www.badger-publishing.co.uk
enquiries@badger-publishing.co.uk

The Biggest Lies Ever! ISBN 1 84424 845 3

Text © Alison Hawes 2006
Complete work © Badger Publishing Limited 2006

Series Editor: Jonny Zucker
Publisher: David Jamieson
Commissioning Editor: Carrie Lewis
Editor: Paul Martin
Design: Fiona Grant
Cover photography: Dragon in a Jar, p18 (c) Allistair Mitchell/Reuters, CORBIS
Illustration: Laszlo Veres and Ian West

THE BIGGEST LIES EVER!

Alison Hawes

Contents

Liar!

We all tell lies sometimes.
Lots of us tell little lies – or fibs.
But some people, like the ones in this
book, tell very big lies!

In 1980, Rosie Ruiz told a
big lie. She ran in a big race.
She came first. But it was a lie!

She just ran the last bit of the race.
In the end, people found out that she
lied, but she did not give her gold
medal back!

Rosie Ruiz 'winning' the Boston Marathon in 1980.

In the 1800s, this man, P.T. Barnum had a circus. He took his circus all over the USA. He made a lot of money from his circus, by telling lies and playing tricks.

He said he had a white elephant - but it was a lie.

Lots of people came to see the white elephant. But it was just an elephant he had painted white!

He said he had a mermaid as well. Lots of people came to see it. But it was just another lie! The mermaid was made out of a fish and a monkey!

Con men!

Con men tell lies. They tell lies that make people give them money!

In the 1920s, there was a UK con man who was very good at getting other people's money.

In 1925, he sold Big Ben to a man for £1,000. He sold Nelson's Column to another man for £6,000. And he sold Buckingham Palace too!

Then he ran off to the USA. There he sold The White House for $100,000.

But the police got him in the end. He went to prison for five years.

$100,000

This con man is from the USA. He lied about the jobs he could do.

He said he was a pilot, a doctor, a lawyer and a teacher – but he was not!

Frank Abagnale

He conned people out of more than $2 million! But the police got him in the end and he was sent to prison.

When he left prison he was given a job. His job is helping to catch con men like himself!

The film, 'Catch me if you can!' was made about him.

Fake photos

People can tell lies, but photos
can tell lies too.

Look at this photo. It is from
the 1900s. Two girls took this
photo of the fairies they saw.

Some people said the photos were fakes.
But lots of people were fooled by them!

In the end, one of the girls said they
had just cut out pictures of fairies and
stuck them on pins!

This photo is from 1934.

It is a photo of the Loch Ness Monster.
Or is it?

For years, people were fooled by
this photo. Now, lots of people think
it is a fake.

They think some people made a model
of a monster and took a photo of it.

In 1936, two men took this photo of
a ghost. The ghost is called the
Brown Lady.

But is it a ghost or is it a fake?

A lot of people think this photo is a fake.
They think it is just one photo on top
of another.

In 1952, this man took a photo of a UFO.

He said he saw 3 men in the UFO.

But a lot of people now think this photo is a fake. They think the man made a model and took a photo of it.

This black and white photo shows some people with an alien.

Or does it? It is a very good photo but is it just another fake? What do you think?

Fake finds

Some people tell very big lies about things they find.

In 2003, a man said he had found a dragon in a jar! But it was just a lie to help him sell his book.

He had a model of a dragon made. Then he put it in a jar and told people he had 'found' it!

In 1869, a giant was dug up in the USA.
At first, doctors were fooled. They said it
was a fossil of a giant man.

It was a fake, but lots of people still
came to see it. The man who made the
giant made a lot of money.

Another giant was found in 1877.
At first, people said it was not a fake,
like the first giant.

But it was! And it had been made by the
man who made the first giant!

In 1912, some men dug up bits of a very
old skull. At the time, people said it was
the oldest skull of a man that had ever
been found. For more than 30 years it
fooled the world.

But in the end, it was found to be a fake.
The skull was not very old and some
bits of it came from an ape.

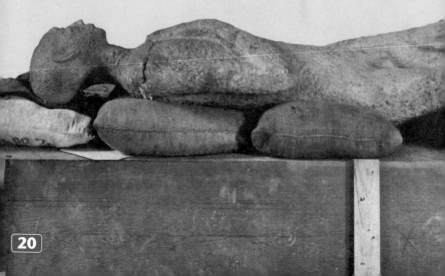

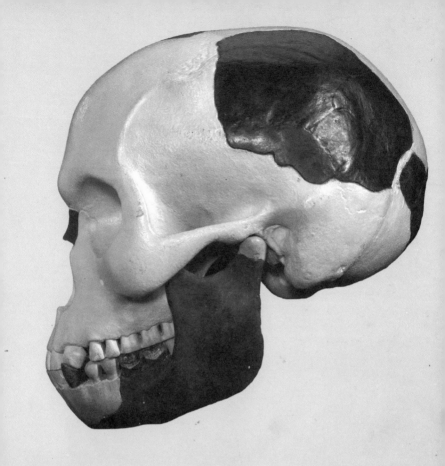

Fooled you!

On the 1st of April, people like to play tricks. They make fools of people by telling them lies!

On April Fool's Day in 1957, there was a film on TV about spaghetti trees.

There are no spaghetti trees! But it still fooled a lot of people.

In 1979, it said on the radio that UK time was running faster than the rest of the world.

It said there would be no 5th or 12th of April that year, so the rest of the world could catch up!

In 2002, some people were fooled by a Tesco advert about whistling carrots.

Tesco said their new carrots had little holes in them. This was so the carrots could whistle, to tell you when they were cooked!

On the 1st of April 2000, people were told they could get slim if they put on socks called 'Fatsox'.

They were told 'Fatsox' could suck fat out of their hot, sweaty feet!

Lies and more lies!

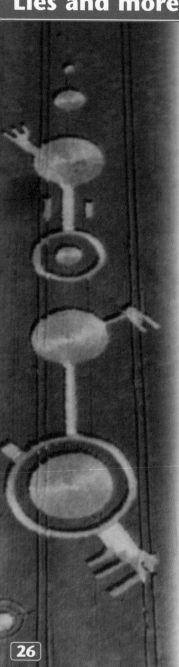

In the UK, in the 1980s, people began to find crop circles like this.

What are they? And who made them? Some people think they are made by UFOs.

A lot of people think they are man-made. They think they are made as a trick!

Some people in the USA
say they have seen a big
ape man, like this:

They call him Bigfoot.
Are they telling
lies? Or not?

And is this a photo
of Bigfoot?

Could it be a fake? What do you think?

In 1981, a man said he had found
Hitler's diaries. But it was a lie.

He sold them and made lots and lots
of money.

But in 1983 he was found out.
The diaries were fakes and he was
put in prison.

In 1998, Burger King put an advert in a US paper. The advert said they were going to sell left-handed burgers for left-handed people!

It was just a big joke, but lots of people wanted to buy them!

In the USA, in 1938, it said on the radio that men had landed from Mars. Lots of people called the police. Lots of people ran away in panic.

But it was just a play!

In the play, men from Mars land in the USA. The play was called 'The War of the Worlds'.

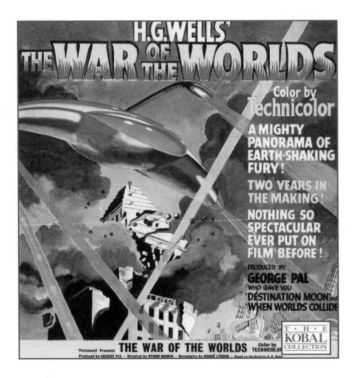

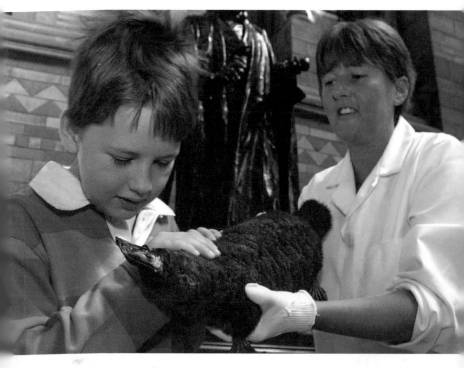

And now for a fake that wasn't a fake!

When people in the UK first saw this animal they said it was a fake.

But it wasn't! They said it was made from a duck and a mole. At first, they called it a duckmole!

But what animal was it?

Index

Cover: Dragon in a jar, p.18 © Allistair Mitchell/Reuters - Corbis.

Images pp.1, 12-17, 26-27 © Fortean Picture Library. Images pp.4-5, 6, 10a, 31 © EMPICS. Image p.10-11 © Dreamworks/Everett/Rex Features. Images p.18 © Allistair Mitchell/Reuters; p.19 © Bettmann - Corbis. Image p.20-21 © Colorado Historical Society. Image p.21a © Natural History Museum. Image p.22 © BBC. Image p.28 © Camera Press. Image p.30 © Paramount / The Kobal Collection.

With thanks to Janet Bord, Fortean Picture Library.